for Jackson and Eleanor,

Merry Christmas 2004

Love, Auntie Sharon and Uncle Jim

# A Goose Named
# GILLIGAN

by Jerry M. Hay
illustrated by Phyllis Pollema-Cahill

H J Kramer
Starseed Press
Tiburon, California

Library of Congress Cataloging-in-Publication Data
Hay, Jerry M., 1946- A goose named Gilligan / by Jerry M. Hay; illustrated by PhyllisPollema-Cahill.      p. cm.
Summary: A river boat captain befriends an injured wild goose that returns year after year to the captain's dock on Indiana's Wabash River.
ISBN 1-932073-09-4 (Hard Cover: alk. paper) 1. Geese—Indiana—Juvenile fiction. [1. Geese—Fiction. 2. Wildlife rescue—Fiction. 3. Wabash
River—Fiction.] I. Pollema-Cahill, Phyllis, ill. II. Title. PZ10.3.H3153Go 2004 [E]—dc22      2003024070

H J Kramer / Starseed Press, P.O. Box 1082, Tiburon, California 94920

Printed in Singapore
10  9  8  7  6  5  4  3  2  1

To Katherine Tuberosa, a good friend to Gilligan and all
animals. On behalf of all the river critters,
thank you Katherine.

J. M. H.

To my husband Jeff.

P. P. C.

Jerry is a river man who lives on the banks of the beautiful Wabash in Indiana.

He loves the river and all of its creatures, and often you will find beavers, herons, groundhogs, and eagles stopping by to pay him a visit. They feel safe with Jerry because he respects their right to come and go as they wish.

Sometimes the water in the Wabash drops so quickly that river mussels are left high and dry on the bank. When this happens, Jerry takes his canoe and goes to rescue them. He knows that mussels are good for the river because they help keep it clean. The river man pitches them back one by one, before the raccoons have a chance to enjoy them for breakfast.

One spring morning, Jerry was returning from just such a mission when he heard a terrible noise. Then he noticed frantic splashing near the shore. "Wonder what's going on?" he thought, as he pulled his boat closer.

At first, he couldn't believe his eyes. A very large goose was in a lot of trouble.

The goose was tangled in a trotline and could not get free. In case you're wondering, a trotline is a number of fishing lines and hooks tied to a main cord and float and then anchored. Fishermen use them to catch fish without using a pole.

The goose was struggling to get away, but the more he fought the worse it got. His feet and wings were wrapped tight in the lines, and the hooks were caught in his feathers. The float was hanging from his neck, and if it hadn't been so serious, Jerry would have laughed out loud.

Jerry quickly tied up his boat, jumped into the water, and swam to where the goose was struggling. This made the goose even more frantic. Jerry swam around the goose, who was hissing, warning him to stay away.

"I know you're really scared, goose, but I can't leave you like this. You'll surely die," coaxed Jerry.

The goose was having none of it, and as the river man cut the lines he was pecked and slapped repeatedly for his efforts. Finally, all the lines attached to the anchor were cut, but there were still lines and hooks wrapped around the goose.

Holding the goose tightly, Jerry explained, "There's only one way to get you free. You and I are going to have to go ashore."

Jerry fought his way up the muddy bank, the goose pecking and slapping, and Jerry talking to him to calm him down. They wrestled in the deep mud and fell back into the river twice. But Jerry was determined to help this stubborn critter. Finally, the river man reached a firm spot on the bank, and he hugged the goose in an effort to quiet him.

"Things will go better if you'd just calm down," Jerry pleaded. "I'm trying to help you."

After what seemed like forever, the big goose stopped struggling. He finally understood that this human was trying to help him.

"Well, that's better," said Jerry, as he carefully removed the last line. Unexpectedly, the goose started talking back. "Honk, honk," he said, as if he understood that Jerry was his friend.

Jerry thought the goose would fly off as soon as he was let loose. Instead, the goose stood in the mud honking, as though to thank the river man.

"You're free now," Jerry explained.

The goose slowly slid into the river and began to thrash about, pecking at the globs of mud that covered him. "What a good idea," Jerry agreed, as he followed the goose into the water.

The two of them bathed and chatted about the predicament the goose had been in. When the goose still didn't leave, Jerry became concerned that he might be injured and couldn't fly.

By now it was getting late, so Jerry swam back to his boat. The goose followed him, swimming in circles and repeating his friendly, "Honk, honk."

"I won't leave 'til I see you fly, but I do have to get along home," explained the river man.

With that, the goose began to run along the water, flapping his huge wings. Then he lifted off. Jerry watched as the goose flew in a circle, honking his goodbyes. The river man waved one last time and headed home.

Neither the scratches and the welts on his head nor the mud and his torn clothes mattered. Jerry was grateful that he had happened along at just the right time.

Early the next day, Jerry was awakened by a now-familiar sound. A loud and insistent honking was coming from the direction of his dock. He threw on some clothes and hurried down to the river, where he was greeted by a visitor. It was the beautiful goose he had saved the day before!

"Well now, it really is nice to see you. I was hoping that I might run across you again someday," greeted Jerry.

"Honk, honk," answered the goose.

They visited for a while before the goose flew away.
The next day the goose came by for another visit and
stayed a little longer. He stopped by every day after
that, staying longer each time. Soon the goose could be
found at the dock almost any time of the day or night.

The goose became quite an attraction, and neighbors up and down the river stopped by to visit with him. Some folks were afraid of the goose, especially when he came hurrying up to the house to greet them with an enthusiastic, "Honk, honk."

"Don't worry, he won't hurt you. He's just being friendly," Jerry would explain.

One day a visitor asked, "What do you call your goose?"

Jerry was startled. The river man never claimed ownership of the goose, since he believed that all wild animals should be free to come and go as they please.

"I call him 'goose' or 'the goose,'" Jerry replied.

"But he has to have a name," insisted his friend.

Jerry thought about that for a minute. "Well, I guess it wouldn't hurt. Why don't you name him?"

She was very pleased to be asked. "I think Gilligan would be a good name for him, and your dock can be Gilligan's Landing."

From that day on, everyone on the river called the goose Gilligan. It didn't take long for the goose to recognize his name, and he would come when called. Some evenings Gilligan would be at his landing honking so loudly that the echo could be heard up and down the river.

During that summer, Gilligan and the river man spent a lot of time together. They could be seen walking along the road, watching the sunset from the landing, and even riding in Jerry's boat. Gilligan would sit on the bow and open his big wings in the gentle breeze.

As fall grew near, large flocks of geese began to fly south. Gilligan called out to them that his landing was a safe place to rest. Jerry watched while Gilligan seemed to be talking to the other geese. The river man wondered whether Gilligan was looking for a flock to join so that he, too, could make the long journey.

Many flocks came and went, and Jerry began to hope that Gilligan had decided to stay for the winter. But one day, a small flock stopped by. As they were getting ready to leave, Gilligan began calling to the cabin with a very insistent, "Honk, honk."

When he reached the landing, Jerry knew what was happening. Gilligan was saying good-bye.

"It's okay, Gilligan. It's always best to follow your nature, and flying south in the winter is what geese do," Jerry said.

"Honk, honk," Gilligan answered sadly.

"I'll miss you, too, big goose. Stay away from those trotlines, and come back to visit any time," advised Jerry.

As they talked, the flock circled overhead, patiently waiting for Gilligan.

That winter was mild. Many flocks of geese landed near the dock, and Jerry waited, hoping that Gilligan would return.

Then one spring morning, he heard the familiar, "Honk, honk." Gilligan was back!

What a great reunion the river man and the goose had. Jerry gave a party that included wheat bread for Gilligan. Friends came to welcome the goose. What no one knew for sure was whether Gilligan was just visiting or was planning to stay.

Well, stay he did. Not only for that summer but for
the seasons to come. Gilligan had found a new home.